TO THE RIVER

BOOKS BY TIM LILBURN

POETRY

Names of God (1986)
From the Great Above She Opened Her Ear to the Great Below
(with Susan Shantz) (1988)
Tourist to Ecstasy (1989)
Moosewood Sandhills (1994)
To the River (1999)

ESSAYS

Poetry and Knowing: Speculative Essays and Interviews (editor) (1995)
Living in the World as if It Were Home (1999)

To the River

TIM LILBURN

Canadian Cataloguing in Publication Data

Lilburn, Tim, 1950-
To the river

Poems.
ISBN 0-7710-5323-1

I. Title.

PS8573.I427T6   1999   C811'.54   C98-932670-5
PR9199.3.L54T6   1999

We acknowledge the financial support of the Government of Canada through the Book Publishing Industry Development Program for our publishing activities. We further acknowledge the support of the Canada Council for the Arts and the Ontario Arts Council for our publishing program.

The author wishes to thank the Saskatchewan Arts Board and the Canada Council for the Arts for financial assistance, and the editors of *Descant* and *Mānoa: A Pacific Journal of International Writing* for publishing versions of some of these poems. He thanks, as well, Don McKay for the loan of his editorial ear and Hilary Clark for a suggestion that led to the title.

Typeset in Minion by M&S, Toronto

Printed and bound in Canada

McClelland & Stewart Inc.
The Canadian Publishers
481 University Avenue
Toronto, Ontario
M5G 2E9

1 2 3 4 5   03 02 01 00 99

怀昭

CONTENTS

I

II

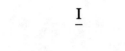

Lay it down, the shimmering glass.
The hooded flickering of the flat is for you, the
                    hooded flame of the hole.
Way out there, don't tell.
You can see winter's limp and unshavedness
                    moving on the hills; it doesn't
                              know where to put its body.
Dark shifts of cranes in the valley.
Be quiet. Move up along the coyote edge, come up
                    along the left-hand bank to the best geese place
                              near the Métis winter camp graves.
Experienced light cruises the clay banks.
You must be this without knowing you are.
The river gleaming with falling down,
                    gold scar of current on its back.
Sandhill cranes on the dock scruffed islands.
A bigger dark comes in from a farther place.

*

Two weeks of thirty-five below and the fat sway of the river
                              is jammed four feet down,
but on the creek between hills, behind
                    beaver dams, ice slumps under snowshoes and
there are no deer tracks.
Fire thrums and lounges godly in the stove.
Big lynx prints behind the hut; heavy
thatch of the Milky Way;
coyotes; the red of the willows
is poor.
Deer coats are poplar ash.

Green ice of the river where a
          hoof has scratched snow crust.

*

Under the wedge of light,
you know nothing.
You'll sing the inside of the snowberry.
A cold with scales heaves up the valley;
    the dark flower of the cold ignites the dark
        flower in the hump of fat things carry.
There is waiting.
You will lay your cheek against the float of the grass.
There is winter in her body;
    there are grains of winter in her body and a low sun.
There is the colour of horror over the snow.

*

I went under the
   earth and the river
gave me a rag, a leg bone to hold.
We looked into one another's
face. Don't say I'm here.
I am feverish with grass.
A dark in things, in wild rose,
       a stalk, a line coming out of the mouth and
curving, is weight, privacy, sleep,
       a cache of fat
the seeable thing sucks on, turns to, and
     lives with.
The bull of the weather moves from here to there,
the purple and the bulge
in the heft of moving, unfallen snow.
The complete moon is still there
when I carry a poplar trunk out of the bush
to cut it by the road.
An inhaled wind moves in things; quiet
      flickers there, receiving a spread of weight.
The dark tower and at its top
      an almost buried light in cold trees.

*

The river is a man who's just ducked into a doorway,
          who's changed his name and lives in the crawlspace.
The river has worn through itself and is turning up its hands.
A man and a dog come across it late in the afternoon
     at a stump-bank near Bohemian waxwings in a cottonwood in
        crouched sun.
Ice plinks and wangs, some thinking
     going on in a room in the castle of the river-ice's private ear,
whale-moan, other-side moan of the ice.
Under the ice, the long hair of what is not there.
Low in the dogwood's throat,
     under dead leaves, the river has its name tied up in some cloth.
The river is widowed.
The rabbit island willows and *Periphyseon*
     and *The Divine Names* are the same thing.
Seeing the willows, their forehead light, you walk into the thicket
     of the book and are poor.
Willow showing red, mild week in January,
     a red that drops its eyes
     when you look at it.

*

Late light, grass-thin and a bone star,
            shimmy of fox tracks beside the black stumble
                  of water, along the river's snow-ice ledge.
The willow has gone into the small room of its redness
where there is no book; the new cold
            lowers a perfect rope to climb into ash.
Way into the burly water, you could hear something.
The woman has looked a pelican descent into me,
                  her weight and her slope,
her weight and slope into me.
You go into the bush and the bush shrugs.
The woman has tipped into me the far corner
            of her eye; I'll build a fire where I am and wait.

Down in the grass, down there.
The dog moves around,
the sky breathes down, its mouth just over us.
Under reeds, a bright, hunched thinking;
swans pull over, over;
heaves of old rain curve round
but are not here.
Quiet in the buck of things;
down in the grass
the lift and the end of light,
        down in the snow-pressed grass.
Rain axes in the air and then a wind – again
tonight the choir-oed, beefy comet.

This afternoon there were ten pelicans skiffing
over the lumpy, tea creek,
ten in my masked ear.
Late ice on the lake, a few yards of loose water at the shore.
Everything is lowered; a smell
        of old snow under the bushes where the brown thrasher was.

*

There are geese over the water, flickering in bad light, something pushing
                                                                through
from the other side; here is desire,
a light around the tongue, world next
to the world, a garden that would appear if the word were found.
What glitters in things is a mountain, it can't be held in the
                                        mouth.
The heavy grasses; night bends from the waist and
                        goes down into them.
The last light is the intelligence, the smallness of
birds in wild berries.
The stars clank up, black-wet weight running
                        on the oil of anticipation.
The geese participate in the boiling dark and they
are a speech of it.

*

The water is a thicket
and a strangeness,
the smoke of the river, the scabbed back.
The ray of the river doesn't bend into your face,
              it's full of the meat of its smell and heaviness.
Tree – a crackling huff of old light.
The water is a thicket of motion and soon
the wheat will be wounded in the fields,
                    it goes straight to compunction.
Sleep is everywhere, early spring,
      things slumped in holes, calm, thinned, snow becomes dust.
A seed of light is building fat and intense
                  in the ground.
Something not yet here will speak for us.

*

Geese on the ice,
         walking;
this is breathing and thinking.
This first lies down in the fields of eternity.
And comes here, hot in its throat, lost, empty.
I live in a hole, I can't help it.
Late afternoon, old grain in wet fields,
         winter-dusty stubble, geese hulking down into it.
You could read by the light of their floating down
                  and understand what you read.
The sun goes into cold pools out there and the
rotting smell of water hushes in
from the stiff fields while there is still
some light, way up and uninterested, in the southwest. In my high
ear, the quaver of the world.
It is the colour of barley water,
                  it rises and dips in a small way that is exhausted.

*

Everything is fallen, everything a soul,
dry stick fire, green water shouldering up among absent-minded,
heavy poplar. I've seen the river; the river is one sleep;
            the forehead, tin-coloured, flexes with guessing. Everything
                                                    is lonely.
In stones, fox, water, violet light, the jounce,
floing at the end of memory, the climb
back up the black fall from thinking, up
the waterfall of rotting into bone, stink, hair, thigh wooing sunlight
in the streaming plummet through air that cooled as
mass blistered in it.
Slow river, coyote-coloured, blue with melting snow.
Dirt river slumping through sugary ice.
The dark lid of the mauve river is falling:
                how little we have.
There is a female light in the branches.

*

The river is a hiddenness, mud-green tree smoking from first darkness you
         could spread out the camp of your life in.
No limit: hold it in your mind and you are weeping.
A grip, a posture of bells.
Coyotes move in the stopped valley, fox through snow,
         one lit judder of prints a plume lifted in the middle of the
                  animal's life.
Later a husky moon, loose bone of a moon.
The world became the world when the light of adoration fell in it
         and it could not stay aloft in invisibility.
Now the river is here, a hand the spirits move.

*

You are good but no blond disc for you in the grass, none, no bone
of light, no little palate or gland of stupid but shining
intelligibility, the pure bride, none, none for you, in the grass prong.
A glacier of night
shoved through the centre of things. Juniper hard with absence.
You are alone in the world: the flab of the river
is anarchic, the water is feathered with ignorance,
a dangerous mirror that makes your face darkness throwing its hair.

*

Almost black light heaves from buffalo leg bones, lichen, a ring
                                                    of stones.
There are geese on the river, walking
                the ice shelf: the erotic world wants more room.
In the night season of winter, dark church with wind outside
                                    it, a limp of water.
Twilight comes from the ground, unwrapped from a rag, all
                                        this dominion has.
The river's breath is a bright elm.
Further in the water, a deeper bark,
                the lack of light so strong you cannot look at it.
The river, head of grass in the chest,
                    wand-stalk,
and the bumble of the horned, chimneying head,
flicking, half sickness, part relief.

Time to talk about cougar light
      of unflexed fields, river turning to straw, light
            curling down from the thinning north, the crane-
coloured paths, about the brown woman
and the star cluster of moles high on her back
and the river.

The sun on the geese-lit flow, city of all
                    that's turned away, the hovering night
lets itself down into the ginger reed water.
I've seen the river in the oldest part of the year,
city of sleep on its back,
the sun in its Egyptian boat,
and it said, look, you are worthless.
And then down through slow valleys of light,
sleeping badly then well in the lost house in bleached sand and old
                cottonwood trees. And then I've come a little
                further along.

There are small planets on Huaizhao's back
and her waist is a crane-coloured path,
a hawk-coloured path.
I have leaves in my mouth,
        it is deer light in the dark grass,
           water of near-night moving in the grass and

the cranes are cheadling to one another on islands of stubbled light and
old bone clay. It's late. There is
the sparrow-coloured woman and the river
and the cougar light of the loose fields.
Small river, eyes lowered,
palomino river, the old world, nothing, a stone
shoulder in the grass.
The crane-coloured paths are as her waist is.
The paths go by the chapped water,
incompetent and more or less certain.

*

Early June;
   behind the ears, rubble.
Now the wheat comes up to you on its shaking legs.
Now you move in the blurred fur of blue light in the large
          ear which is the darkness of the garden.
Small ache of the new moon over ungerminated peas
                  uncovered in their trench.
Stars now over the garden, a glow like thinking smudging it, onions
  first inches, thinking with a head-ducking, coppery thunder cat-slow
    sewn into it over the beginning wheat.
You are in someone else's clothes walking at a slant to the gold
                  momentum.
Thinness lets you walk through the trees.
A small purple strip has been hauled out and hit with ropes,
               something has been lifted out.
The garden looks at you. Both you and it washed
    in the blood of not being seen.

*

Don't say you've heard this.
I'm in a limping house that's breaking up,
          floating on the star river. Mineral light
over the big-armed, turned-away ground.
The place just stands under the fat quaver of northern lights.
Pigweed closed in, wattle of morning bird song – ask it
                                    to lead the country
     and it'd tie a stone round its middle and jump into deep water.
In my hand, the clean and glittering
weapon of doing what the light eventually tells me.
Sunflowers, peas, wheat, spinach,
carrots are up.
They are the dragon again, promising
          obedience, eddying muscle of the other side;
they will live with us and living with us
means letting themselves be fleeced by the beam thrown
by the tightness of our hearts, means their eyes on
the hollow just below our throats, the blood-jump.

*

The long striding dirt kicks into
big, important felt boots and is gone
in a grainy, moth's-back dusk
out past the waxy light of petunias,
war light, light with no mind
the river forgets up over the rise.
It goes into the mountains,
it tends sheep; what it eats is what
it breathes of the clotted dark of extreme distance.
Last summer I lived in the grove of her skin.
A bear's ear of new potato appears on the ground.
The eyes of everything sharp and young on my hands
                                    in the morning,
I walk in the garden and am admired.

*

Heavy fall of three-week
male wheat, a matinée forelock. It did this
by itself.
It looks up because it thinks this is beautiful, but can't
see over the anvil forehead. It can't sing.
Its body is an olive-gold cloth it doesn't know what
to do with laid across its arms.
The flavour of the indifference of the bend of the iris
stem, the meal
of its carelessness – the small penis of light in
            me stands on end and stays that way all day.
Everything thick-faced with green,
            first stars a few crazy people round scrawny fires in the hills.
Late now, just a little light in a thicket where no one
comes, high, poisonous – the grass flattens its
mirrors and in the fresh dark in the tall
stalks there's a room where everything can slowly open its eyes.

*

Pale elm tangle and winter-sheened brome grass, the back stutters.
A hump of black stuff under
                    the earth steers the water.
Knowledge flickered among hummocking caribou
            antlers further north, herd turning, but here swallowed,
                kept low.
The river is a new bone, dirt-haired, just out of the body, an
            animal on its own at dusk.
It rolls back its walrus fat and is still fat a long way down.
It thinks;
it's been rubbed by the grass and is light-headed; nothing
                            comes to it.
It's unmeant; it says, look, the new
                moon and a star above its lower belly.
In the chokecherries' creaking dark, the river
                    jerks its bristled eye.
The river's muscled nose; the river
            moves up its army where we sleep,
where a hand simply feeds a fire, along that losable road.
It robs just past the edge of plenty.
It stays behind while the light in everything moves forward.
It lives in a small room.
Its ears are cold-burnt down to the skull.

*

You'll go away and it's there,
               the river doesn't know you.
The water, a long, furred ear, and
at the end of hearing a small bright house.
No one owes the river money.
The hammer arm, bear teeth, gummy
               eye sick with winter grass: nothing owed
here.
It's missing parts, old voice
   with a hole in it, cluttered as magpies.
Long cold.
Across diseased ice, willows the
               shade of a far, childhood sleep.

*

Dark land quaking, horned water giving off a far light.
I am hooded, cupped, down there hustling along the edge
with the mongrel water.
The smoke of distance there, winter-powdered grouse shit, wolf willow.
The river's shrug has made a plain around it,
   a flat around it lit with sluffed, blank water, the river which is
      played on a three-strings-broken guitar, which doesn't care, which is
         whooping its face off in its long hair against the wall of its room.
Camped out alone, late spring night, cold light.
Slack with owls, the river,
bareassed, a few twigs,
laughable, depressed.
Don't tell anyone. We'll live in second-hand clothes
in a house that's snuck up beside the water.
Out there, all the bones hum, a ringing the grass
         touches in.

*

You eat the bread of seeing, you are covered and set over there.
    Whale flukes of elms, woody ice, dark chimes in the bodies of birds
    heard through the eye's skin.
The bear-robe river and the breathing, after-supper light
              have rubbed their bony scent against you
and now you are someone with just twigs and grass
coming out of him. A shoulder like a magpie's nest.
Furred scat, a golden wind priding along punk ice,
        dismembering, corpse ice.
Hawk-bellied land, you'll go along it; you are married, going along.
In thin April morning snow, frogs.
The river is shrugging its charcoal ice, scab ice, the water's
       manchurian eyes, craning cheekbones,
            the belly.
You like the deer, their chokecherry turds and the sump
smell of unmuscled fields, elms leaning into their faces
and the new boy's-body heat getting up
beside the oldest snow. Juncos down there.

Big weather coming in along the valley that stands back, that will
                     not be first.
Birds on the sick ice; a thick-tongued black
sway in the air with no message coming up the valley.

Low-voiced blue stuttering of last light in spinach
and over-watered beans.
In a bearded wind, the river's at your hip.
The river stubs itself into a further, cormorant night.

The secrecy of the grass's jewelled
summer waist – say
nothing, it says.
The kingdom of heaven in the grass
pulling a
forgottenness toward itself with a full-hands'
erotic gravity: it knows
the way and takes it.
The secrecy of the coyote rising
on its two legs to see
and the secrecy of the half-year fawn
moving through grass and near, shadowing
their off-centredness,
the lacquer dark under the nail of things
you could pray to but is too wobbly and floating off.

The swollen grass is a night
sway in the eye,
a jewelled waist; it

breathes the light of your face all into it.

You'll sleep on the ground
behind the shack of the river.

*

Good self: kiss my ass.
Nothing will come near,
not grass, nothing.
In the grass, it's nightfall,
dragonflies planted in the thick light.
Quavering, low, blurred, hunched light, light in a mouth;
and green-blue dragonflies held up in it.
The eye draws its tongue along the bulge of mind in the
                              collapse of the river's flow;
in the throat an endless mountain.
I'll go back to the water, a place
            there, pressed-down grass,
      I have some nudity there.
I am a shrug tipping through willows, the river bright with
                  wandering off, bright with failure.

Big doubt at the end of the grass flick,
chunk of cement, an illness. Something will happen,
         it will be both expansion and breaking down.

*

Your face is the river breathing in it.
This is pathetic.
Wolf light of its going and forgetting under your skin.
Vodka shine of near winter in the north;
                              there are yellow tamarack in it.
There is a lying-down here with you,
              a silvery lying-down in the thin
                   cave of looking,
the flat, black stone of the back-of-its-head-to-you river
                              on your stomach.
All you could know and you do not know it.
Just before night, a scoop-
              gut moon a little under flattened snow clouds, coyote,
                   off-to-one-side moon.

*

Rain claw to the north,
        the river clumps in near, all
                nose, pushing the done grass.
The fire cleans itself, curls in.
The river, a ledge of faces running just under it.
Oxtail flick of having nothing and staying where you are.
No flavour in the way the water bends, nothing in the mirror;
                it's inside the pelt of a coyote someone shot and skinned.
Animal flow, sandbars hovering
up and late geese, near winter sun on the bullhead curve;
I'll wear a hat of dogwood sticks.
Out where everything is, willow sleep
and then a goosefeather moon,
        flinch of light almost grown in.

*

You can tell the river is old when there are geese on it, their
        swallowed kerosene shine, the idea of
            migration a deadweight, smoke-haired package of sewn
                sailcloth they've never opened that they keep with them.
The light in them is just one and further away, down
                    hallways.
Just one in the whole big house of geese.
The animal of the near-dark valley
        has never said anything. No
one remembers it's an animal, so it isn't dead.
The fat order of geese near dark, moving to the island, one blurred
    one fumbling into place in the slipstream, then over the iron bridge.

*

It isn't here, don't think about it, the thrown shoulder
                              covers it.
Thick-skulled with sandbars, old yelling
            with a tongue stump, straw river, wolf
river, the abandoned eye, hidden, turning away from the light
and moving off, a joke, shallow, then blundering
down, islands blind with diamond willow, blind with snake
grass, frozen goldenrod, this way, then its purpose
knuckles under, pointless slipping belt, thick
drunk, chuddering, a falling house,
colour of a dead hornet's nest.
I am breath slag, something nude in me.
The river falls off a moving cart then nothing.
The body of the woman is lodged in my throat.
The moon is a small possible fever a long way off.

*

Huaizhao, listen, I lay down everything
and go into the blackness floating under the earth,
this is ignorance and burning floating under the earth and I
move along this edge of thrombic blackness, white candle of what must
be done in my hand.
I go to it, orchard of shadow, wolf-echo;
there's the world of the world,
a loping, flameless burning, borderless intent, blue and driven
under the earth.
The river under or behind the river, the eloquent
night in the night.
There's snow on the ground, late November, deer
darkening in dogwood bush.

The deep singing in this thinking about darkness,
this thinking under the ground in a frost robe, this is breathing, building
a fire and sitting before it, the bush around.
Plucking the lowest breath, bowing it with sleep.
The ignorance
and burning of the cloud under the earth, the moving,
its scent of near amnesia.

*

I've come late and find my place in the choir rustling
and am shown the line of darkness we are now singing and
                    have been singing from mid-November on. Here we are.
And I take up my part which is the bull's penis singing
                    out, which is amaryllis,
which is the shoulder of summer lifting in the steam of summer,
bronze instrument for weighing the sky weird in my mouth: the shape of
                    heaven is the shape of earth.
All around us, accompanying, there is ice suddenly appearing on the river.
I am what the darkness likes.

The river sits in the blood chair.
The dolphin plain stumbles out a breathing,
                              barely given-off light,
the intelligence of a block of salt.
The river sits in the blood chair,
        its desire lifting and coming back down to it in its own early-
                              December smoke.
Dull stub of receiving light on the plain going toward crumpled
        snow hills then toward the red-gold mountains.
The river is the unlit fat.
Neither ascending nor descending, it doesn't care.
It is the flat part of looking where the breath is even.
A large cooling animal.
The river sits in the blood chair,
            its desire lifting and coming back down in its winter smoke.
An animal standing out there,
        cooling from the distances, smoke of all
                that it has done coming
from it, dead-green around it.

*

You go to the river; it wants to live in a hole; it
wants to be curled in, nude river, grizzly-backed water.
You look at the river and you know it.
The river is ashamed of the tight, loud light
saluting from its torso; it stands a little from its bank, blurred
                                    animal, no greater, no less.
You go there and are walled into nothing
and lie down.
A darkness worms forward and up in you.
You are walled into nothing, the hips, the quiet of the river nearby;
                                    you will not get up.
The river is a bone, the river a drift, the tilt
of silty glow in the head.
Late spring, berries work from flowers, bodies fall from light.
A rufous towhee skates tree station to tree station, raising
                        the sword of its voice.
You examine yourself by the gleam of the motion
of things that move. No
blame.

*

You don't know anything.
The river sees you, a weight, in evening, in its forest eye. You'll
live in a hovel in there, way back. You say to the bull eye you love the
                              quaver-skinned woman, love that one.
The river's stamina breathes looks into your chest,
straight in, adoring; let them come, let the light of you go to it.
Seeing is moving in terrifying skin.
A big light lifts from the naked wheat:
          if we take off our clothes emptiness starts
             to polish our skin from the inside, the pitch of this
                 light building until the knife-edge
                 of it is held to our throats.
A light bucks in the wheat and lifts above it.
Not human but full of acclamation like the idea of proportion.
While you sleep everything creeps forward in the sheath of its beauty,
hawkweed, juniper, looking neither left nor right,
each flux lubricated by your not seeing it,
everything as you walk sending out its tongue
to meet your tongue.

*

Her leafy hands are part of a choral attention
that includes the flute of evening, its flamingo,
pepper-sauce light and the secret wheat,
the blue hump of the hill in its milky air
and the prisons west of the city
under beating stars where canola
dawns and dawns, floating out against the smoky
                    reptile weight of the prisons.
Out there black motes of the absolute muster
                    in the pod. The prisons' salt tents huff and clench
against stakes of bone. The hills there are dead animals.
But it's her hands and the breathing in the subversive, cornered
    wheat that turns with less back to you, ears up and polite, parliament
                    of the dark world.
Her skin, late-afternoon dust from an earlier dynasty,
                    old hills north of the capital, lift of thick palm.
The flexed tree of her looking.
Down into the afternoon of her side,
                    there you go,
                    you're on your way, holding some light, an antler,
to look at her evening feet in palace bedrooms of canola
                    that are so far to the west almost no one hears of them.

*

You go down into the small room in the swede saw, into the long
                day in that room where you cook some
                vegetables late in the afternoon
                and eat them.
You are under the earth; there are
                grass roots and amplitude, you are
                breathing.

*

You ride a bird into the wide, long black,
     an oriole into the green cloud weight, it rolls through
        cottonwoods, its body is an eye opening;
            you are shaved to breath.
Into the quiet listening-to-you, world-big
            turned-to-you; no one comes near you or sees
            you.
You lie down carefully here, you will look around.
A sway of sleep in what is bright,
     the old sleep hills,
           mumbled, self-correcting hills.
The day falls in on itself.
A darkness comes out of
     the grass. It comes toward you.

*

You are so tired now.
Everything is burning inside itself.
This is the fire of turning away, the fire of
          farness let in.
Late August, sandhill cranes at 20,000 feet
               in the airless, white end of the sky.
Tick of ash columning in grassblade; even
     the wind in the throw of its gleam is slowly
     on fire.
In the afternoon, the moon comes.
Asters out in the fields
               and the shivering wall of the wasps' attention.
Everywhere the faces of things pouring the gold of what
               they are into an unseeable place.
Light lives above its body now, light looks
          on what it's done, what it can't get back to.
Blue dragonflies flux and heave in the narrowing glow.
You will never read all there is
in the library of this dark.

*

The river, a ledge of faces running just under it.
Oxtail flick of having nothing and staying where you are.
You are hefted by the swimming machine of light
                    in the grass's seeing,
hefted and let down, the grass's flesh swing
                       toward you, a leaning.
The meat and the shrug
and the mane of the river, smell of dead skin
under its pelt.
Its muscle and hover, its exhalation, it lies down
                     in rye flats with the eye.
In itself and elsewhere, the river a feathered thing.
I'll go down there.
I'll take the gold body
that is quarter-full in my body, thinness rushing
                  to its edge, a building voice,
and put it in the grass.

*

I'll lie down here
bending stalks of light,
fronds, seedheads. It's in the long
            turn away in things, willow island centre under a storm's
                fist, a place inside birds, ground cloud of foxtail, a long way.
You sleep your way there; at last you're
                on a slope like the back of an angry dog; it's
                dark, there's no other way to come at this, no
                    knowing, you ride out on the tongue of desire. It's been
so long since we've been here
where the light is falling.
Let's go down there
singing.
Singing is taking away everything
then standing in the mud of light,
willow light, poor as that.
There's the smoke moon, the mange
moon. It's come
            up over the stupid and the empty grass.
Beside us, the heaviness of all things turning.

*

I want to be found here
after four winters, naked, drinking with the deer. It's the continent
and the age of dusk. The odd stones are shafts of black attention. Saltflats,
foxtail, the mauve sky shivers with snow geese slackening back from the
blinding fields.
I don't amount to much.
This is a song, you sing it, then become it, the work of God.
I want to go back under the moon, poor as the trees.
Want to be found and seen with this one breast in my mouth.
You are your bones and the bones of the late sun are around you.
There's the grass, penile nod
of grass, weightless,
roots in wet stone. The eye stutters here, there,
first snow chitters down.
I'll live in a room in the green wave of the skin and it'll come here.
The smell of holiness, the smell of loving, snow-iron bottom of the wind, I'll
know I'm near,
and then, out of smoky light, there'll be a weak path through aspens and
down to the water.
I'll be thinner, whiter, heels
wedged against buttocks; I'll be waiting, bent down, listening.
I'll smell of the spice of rotting poplar, blond smell, the bread
sunlight turns into, worked into hide.
I'll tip forward, there I'll be, a far thing, angled away, drinking.

*

Sour poplar at the edge of the tree island, watered
by starlight, hidden, gravel-pale, going into winter.
The starvation of each tree lives next to it and the tree
                    eats the body of its ghost, that's
how they live, tree and ghost, side by side, no love but necessity. Standing
by them, you are standing by a small snowmelt stream in the Rockies.
I'll sing something, old iron.
Iron with snow in it.

Distance thrums, it's full of nerves
– over the flats,
the roll of it south over the big grass,
you feel like lying down watching it, over
alkali lakes, coulees, lost hills,
bone-coloured rivers,
and the geese are letting this black stream
into themselves, letting it roll and tangle in,
they can't help it, this filling them with wind and night
and what is between the early winter stars.

My tongue sleeps in its clothes down in the asphalt dumps
and weeds by the river.
It is not light but it will stand here for a while.

Sex flickers in the darkness of things, stones, river
bend, willows, an oil gleam, light
of something moving, oyster-glimmer, indifferent, turning toward you,
turning away.

So nothing will ever be enough.
A bruise of sky is shunting into place the high, fleshy
                              silence of
snow; under this, deer-coloured grass and
cranes lifting, a little wind moving four feet off the ground,
air light and water light on the waiting tundra swans.
The water smells like a hole filled with old leaves
              where you once might have lived.
The water smells of you.

II

MARRIAGE AND AGRICULTURE

1

You are embarrassed by this.
Captured, bright-mouthed,
            volt-pectoralled man, and taken to hell.
There pinned, inoculated with the bottom of the universe.
Now it's possible, now what couldn't happen does.
Now it does, great eros turning itself
                    in a way that makes it want to be sick
but makes it think it is contralto-ing out
a shape past the edge of things,
        prolapsing a leaping elegance past
            everything, unmappable, that turns and kills all earlier desire
                        with its beautiful hands.
It is in flames. An eloquent standing.
Now a steep weight in the torso turns toward the world.
You turn toward marriage and agriculture.
You turn toward the grain holding the wide
            afternoon of light.
You can walk right into darkness now,
                right into blood and children.
Now the weight of late afternoons in the fields
                    is the true soil of the groin.
Now the anti-wobble poise in the lilac skin turns
            with blinding slowness toward marriage and agriculture.
This is love and sorrow, this

is not being worthy.
On tingling hinges the terrible black swing.
Now it turns in air heavy with a density of momentum,
                    that perfume of assent,
on night-hinges, water-hinges, a swing
full of frightening inadvertence, animal,
forest in you, what
you smell like deep in.

Love is my weight, says Augustine, and
                    it pillows him to where he must be.
The backs of hills, horse hills, are like grief,
are grief.
Give up, they say, give up. The birds ride.
Something in the cloud of skin turns
                    toward the lovely things.
But Augustine later, in his burning, in his burning –
          the shining man out alone in the wilderness of multiplicity.
Now that being settled, now that it is clear that this is
                    not a sweet return but a killing and a coming
                         out alive through the killing,
something in the bone-dark wheels with
          blinding irrevocability outward toward the light-holding things.
You are going out of yourself like animals
                    returning to the loneliness of what they are.

2

The world is tall, it lives away.
If only you were pure.
Your breathing's not right.
Night leans its shoulder into your lung.
Looking for potatoes under the sand floor at the end of winter.

If only you were pure.
You are half burnt down with insomnia.
You'd like to think breath's the bearing wall.

3

I will go into the stone and
       hide in the singing, camouflaged.
I will go into the stone and stand up.
I will hide in the bell of her black hair,
       in the rain of her hair I will breathe inside a room.
Through the terrible door, the long dark reaches –
                      open country.
Who cares? I'm not going *there*, not now. Now I'll
lie down in the flesh of the smell of the river.
It's lost, I'm lost.
With me is the cat, nude smell of her hair.
I'll speak to no strangers now.
I found this woman in fixed stone,
         red cord round her neck, our bedclothes damp,
ripe with forest. What do we do, what do we do all day?
We imagine nothing.

4

I go down the slope of her voice, into villagers, mist, beneath
                              trout-lily-coloured hills.
I see it all now, evening star showing, a lostness entering what is.
I am moving near the range lip, my progress is tassled and there are
flutes of dusk, I love myself and my love gathers a procession
ahead of me
and behind me and I am in a red sedan chair of silk.
This is the valley where I was born.
I am to marry the night and the cool idling up from the reservoir.
My right hand is raised, this is how things are.
As they are meant to be, landscape where everything's counted
                              and effortless.
A force that is like giving up fevers through the strange grasses
and apricot trees.
This will defend the passes and so we can sleep.
I travel into the heavy fall of light of her shoulders and stomach,
                    I will go into the music,
the horse-picking-its-way-down-a-grade of her skin.
I will arrive in the world.
I am hidden, I am visiting a tree, I have come tired as a rock
                              here.
Inside me glitters unaccountably a careful knowledge
          of how and where to plant the new corn.

5

You turn toward the bulging spawn-brightness of the massed
things, big-stomached, lit inside.
You do not want this.
So heavy, such heavy light, seeing
                is depletion, a faint life.
A namelessness blooms through the arms: I do not want to die
                       without moral weight.
Thus consciousness returns to the home of the darkness
                of grass. So small.
I will think now of Huaizhao's apricot breasts,
        of dusk in her valley, spring corn in clay.
The building keeps burning itself down
      as if something careless, strong
             wanted us to become virtuous.
The grass in June is alert with fury.

6

O long grass of inattention.
Rocky moths, night, new moon, July.
The river is below, wearing itself
        out, going off alone again to sniff alongside
        a higher range of exhaustion it alone hears,
        the shape it feels forming, dark palace, in its mouthings.
The night, too, will go on, fine thing, but further, forever, so I
        can let it go, taking care of itself.
I step to one side, the sound of the temple bell under
rotted leaves
in the valley below Hong-luo Mountain 8,000 miles to the west,
now in high day,
hunches low in my ear. Remember me.
The wind here, in dusk, in vetch light, loam
        of light, wind full of black flecks, wind from it could be
                anywhere, north most likely, a little
                west, full of bruises, wind full of the metallic
taste of never arriving home.

7

Poplar luff of her belly,
dragonfly of her belly.
Over the bull-necked water, evening, in the strangled curve
                of two pelicans, their weight-hounded curve, six-inch
iron wheels
                        roll on one another,
but nothing opens, and the light over the river
does not open; it could say your name, but it does not open.
What calls blocks the way.
You would like to seed something in this
plain of aroused sediment, river light, soft middle of your tongue,
its fragrance would be your face.
But there is no home. Here the light is determined.
No collapsing into it.
Nothing this way at all.

8

You turn with a bright slowness toward the single world.
You are ashamed.
The river worms from the eye
pounding black drums.
It goes away, the river is quilled with dark, it
                          smells of antelope under guard hair,
the river goes into mud.
There are antelope near it, the river, poor in a frightening way.
Slab of its neck, you feel like drinking yourself crazy.
At night, alone with itself, it flies round the world, long
                          colours writhing.
The river smokes in morning, it is a genius.
Whoever wants the river can't help being pathetic,
                          it's too far out in the unbidden world.
You want this, just try not to be pathetic.
Think of something jumping with distance, then let eros
cancel the idea with the momentum of eros. That's where
the river is, out that way, out there.

9

I live near the water, the only thing near that smells of the end,
                               clay water.
No children, no brightness stumbled from me.
Gouged clean by the velocity of a small clear point, I've got
                           nothing to say.
I'll put gold seeds in the loose white earth soon, flake of night
             falling in my hand, or where's the weight, stone pillow
                        for a life to rest? The river
is the darkness of the indifference of what is most intimate.
Small moths over the mum water's stagger carry double
their weight in early-September light.
The sun now rots at the edge of the world.

10

Far into her nakedness, a lilac-leafed dark.
Lay down everything, lay it down.
You will watch and the light of the world will herd away from
                                                                you.
It will go because it loves you.
With unanimity and mass, gone.
And then, ahead, later, the hawk-belly curve of the shine
and accommodation of things
will be given and you will know it.
I miss my dog, her gravelly gold in dead grass.
I want to stand up, light pouring from me.
I bow to the stone, I touch the tree.
After a night of first frost, a rubbery vibration in the steep last
green of what is there as if someone
inside had been singing.

11

Chokecherries are where the past in late August
comes and lives in their caves of darkness; beyond them is
nothing, events
have built up and ended here; chokecherries are the debris
of all earlier things, a version of all; they woo summer's
opulent rot into absent-minded bodies, rounding it off their
own way, because they are at the moment the edge of the world.
What they do now loves the hill slope, nothing more is needed.
Above the ground's blond heat,
their sleep is armour, single purpose.
Because of this generosity, laying its voice beside it,
a blue quaver lives under the human skin, a hill line, a
farness attentive like a waiting animal. There, under skin,
a speech running beside the shambling completeness of
chokecherries and the pang of crickets in grass.
Now clay light, the light of her skin in the maroon-red dress, the
light which is the confidence the rotation of the earth throws off,
this light now comes out of the forest because everything is safe
and moves down to the river.
The blueness under the human skin is open now, though the
climb into it is dangerous. There are pale lights in that dark rim.
We live behind a gate of boards and grass.
The corn is in tassel, my tongue moves, gleaming orbit of the small
                                    planet in her, there
are turquoise veins in her thighs.
I am walking in hills in an edgeless wind, muddy current in my
                                    tongue.

Her body is mansion and dusk, in her belly a bowl of distance,
her feet in tasselled corn, where bits of night
never leave.

12

I miss the world, I sing for it
                in a room.
Deer, cottonwood, moon.
Her berry-dark neck.
The tottering river, deer; o grave of the ear,
                     o grave deeper in.
A man leaves his head on lifting ground, he's
lonely for the river's sleep, for green afternoons
under elms to come to him and lie down beside him all his days
                                   in the grass.
He'd claw-hammer his heart,
jerk it over the wall and
follow it home. There is no home.

13

The river lives in shadow-pools of tall stones.
It is immortal and long-haired, its fingernails grow.
Small feathers of impulse kiss from its stalk, it
lives in these colourless leaps from itself, it tends a small
garden of bells.
Slop-bellied, radiant, left-slumped river, the thrown world,
holds a pale green stone fire in its arms always;
it is oiled with inertia, wolf-
coloured, laying small pubis mounds of clay.
The light-ghosted cottonwood, the one
near the unfolding water, the light idling in the cottonwood,
suddenly stands up, stands up, palms raised at sunset, stands up.
I don't know anything.
A towering generosity in things being where they are.
Far along, north, spruce coming into aspen, half a mile in
from the river, an antler in grass leaking light in barely lit grass.

14

I sway in the light of her speaking,
in the skin ray.
The last harrier is belly-weighted
       with a compulsion to the earth. I'll go to school in inertia.
Flat, grasshoppered heat sleeps from cut fields.
The harrier calms the grasses polishing; the bright
           slide licking, licking, a calling to light heaves and falls
                    of grass by intensity.
Edgeless fixity, dagger-glint.
Sun the colour of gravel, thistle in head.
Everything is gathered by eccentric gravities starting up
like flowers no one can remember planting –
female goldfinches clenching along the river in wolf willow,
              the river filling with dust.
In the abstraction above sky, a swallowed saxophone flumping,
sandhill cranes, their intelligence
            and the new moon suddenly late in afternoon over
                         whitening ground.
Who knows why heaven dislikes what it dislikes?
Hawkweed and aster.
Letters come from the frontiers.
There are coyotes in the valleys, ganging
at sunset and dawn, blood-magneted, their serrated voices
cutting something badly and with insistence.

15

The river blows a black, hoof-bright horn.
It wears a cap of dead owls.
The river is empty and a shiver of bronze bridles.
A sandstone light inside the river and in
geese heaving down upon it, careless pewter
love, a closed, small
distant heat. Grain everywhere quiet, there, with itself;
other things happen, dusk is an arousal over yolky fields.
Nothing leads
to it, nothing comes away. Flyways
open, quavering ghost
rivers of premonition, a breathing and a light.
To know this light and be human would feel like fever
                                    and the need to sleep.
Cottonwoods by the river like burning men,
                        the light over the river is erect,
the light over the river.
Dead buffalo stones keep in the green-grey flow,
and the banks of the river are bone and on the clay-bone dead
poplar washed up.
A touching and settling of things now at the end.
Lime algae leaning away from important clouds
emperoring northwest in last sun, a red appearing in reeds, the
many loving the one, the weight of all things found equal, the
dark island swallowing itself, juniper berry
first to enter the night, some dogwood just now

blooming against a cliff of purchaseless dark, blundering
                    toward last moths and copulating dragonflies curving
on the final lip of habitable light.

16

It carves genius, it carves light-love;
no eyes but a hyperbolic nose.
Dragon-blade, single, body-length muscle.
It wants a shape inside itself clean enough to lie down
                    with sorrow.
It tastes the winds coming from what is
                not there, a music and an architecture
                bright with terror.
Desire rows out again and again.

The river feathers deeper into exhaustion;
                it grows more and more blond, soon
                there will be no memory in it at all.
The woman is folded into me between ribs, fists, and
                lower arms, black
thickness of bees, plump eruptive shade,
a big fish lying among stones in
the long shafts of dark in June.
The bouldered river, sullen drunk.
It is not here, but on a horse northwest of here
        looking at snow coming out of a purple cloud, moving
        toward it, snow, first snow.